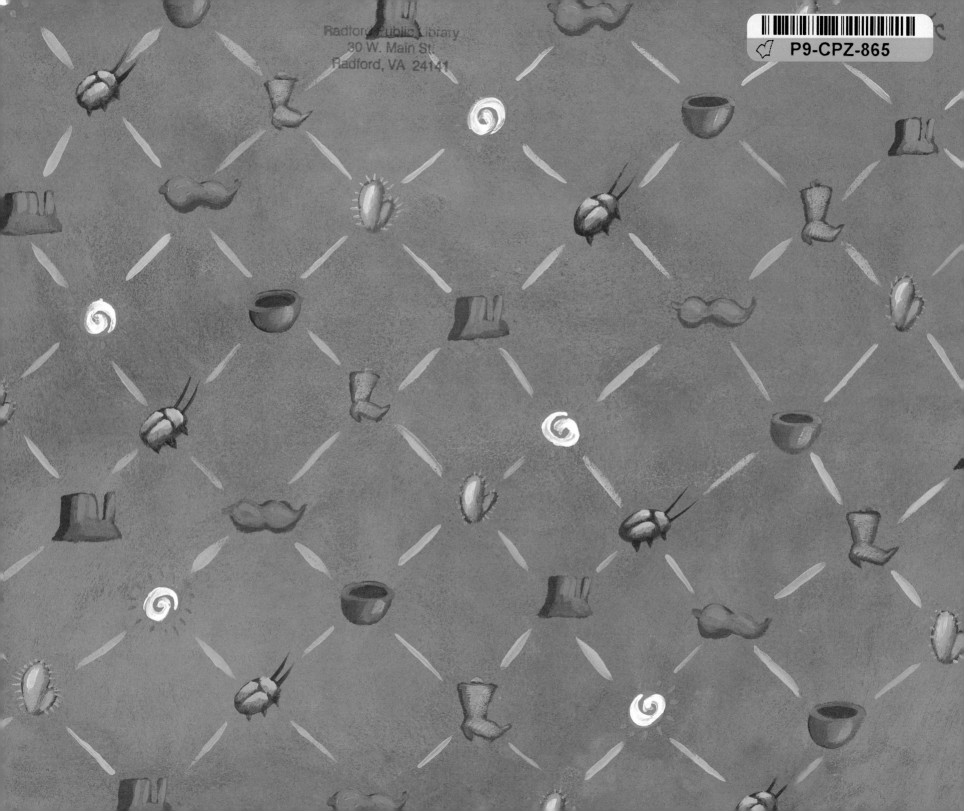

# Armadilly Chili

Helen Ketteman

ILLUSTRATED BY
Will Terry

Albert Whitman & Company, Morton Grove, Illinois

Library of Congress Cataloging-in-Publication Data

Ketteman, Helen.
Armadilly chili / by Helen Ketteman ; illustrated by Will Terry.
p. cm.
Summary: In this Texas-style adaptation of a traditional folktale, a
tarantula, bluebird, and horned toad refuse to help an armadillo
prepare a batch of chili but nevertheless expect to eat it when it's ready.
ISBN 0-8075-0457-2 (hardcover)
[1. Folklore.] I. Terry, Will, 1966- ill. II. Little red hen. English. III. Title.
PZ8.1.K54Ar 2004 [398.2]—dc22 2003014855

The design is by Will Terry and Carol Gildar.

For more information about Albert Whitman & Company,
visit our web site at www.albertwhitman.com.

For my quilting group, whose friendship is as warm and comforting as a bowl of hot armadilly chili—
Bev, Cheryl, Judy, Linda, Nini, and Margaret.

—H.K.


For Zack, Aaron, and Seth.

—W.T.

Miss Billie Armadilly skit-skat-skittered down the lane.
"A blue norther's a-blowin' and my old, cold bones are rattling
for a pot of hot armadilly chili," she said.

She was gathering beetles when her
tarantula friend, Tex, came by.

"Hey, Tex! I'm making a pot of armadilly chili!" said Miss Billie. "How's about tapping your toes this way and helping me gather a boxful of beetles?"

Tex wiggled his long, jiggly legs. "Shucks, Miss Billie. I'm going dancing today."

"Then I'll fill my box with beetles myself!" harrumphed Miss Billie.

When she finished, Miss Billie headed for her garden.
She was picking jalapeño peppers and chipotle chilies when Mackie
the bluebird swooped down from his bush.

"A cold norther's a-blowin', Mackie! How's about whistlin' us a tune and helping me pick a peck of peppers for my armadilly chili?" asked Miss Billie.

"Not today, Miss Billie," said Mackie. "I'm shaking my tailfeathers to the movie."

Miss Billie snorted. "Then I'll pick a peck of peppers myself!"

After she finished, Miss Billie scurried to the prickly pear cactus patch and started chippity-chop chopping.

Her friend Taffy, a horned toad, looked down from her rock.

"How's a gal 'sposed to concentrate with such a racket going on?"

"Taffy! I'm chopping cactus for my armadilly chili!" said Miss Billie.
"How's about helping me chop a chunk or two?"

"Can't you see I'm lacing my skates? I'm skating the day away," said Taffy.

Miss Billie's face turned red. "Then I'll do the chopping myself!"
When her basket was full, Miss Billie hurried home.

She began to fix her armadilly chili.

She mixed and stirred and cooked, and stirred
some more. Soon the armadilly chili bubbled on the stove.

Miss Billie was carrying out the trash when Tex tottered up.
"Howdy, Miss Billie," said Tex. "It's a mighty cold night and I could smell
that armadilly chili a-cookin' all the way home from the dance hall."

Miss Billie plunked the lid on the trash can. "I have a saying, Tex. 'No workin' with Billie, no sharin' the chili!' I'm afraid you danced yourself out of dinner, cowboy."

"Whoa! I'm sorry you feel that way, Miss Billie!" Tex whirled around and hurried home.

Miss Billie stood there feeling sour as a scorpion. Suddenly, Mackie blew in on a cold breeze.

"It's a rough wind a-blowin', Miss Billie. But I could face it if I could warm myself with a bowl of that fine-smelling armadilly chili."

"Sorry, Mackie," snapped Miss Billie. "No workin' with Billie, no sharin' the chili! Maybe remembering that movie will keep you warm."

Mackie's tailfeathers drooped, and he flew away.

Miss Billie went inside to stir and taste her chili. It needed a little something. She dropped a few more peppers in the pot.

Ding-dong! Miss Billie answered the door. Taffy stood there shivering. "I'm f-freezin', Miss Billie! Could I beg a bowl of your hot armadilly chili?" she chattered.

Miss Billie shook her head. "Land sakes, Taffy!
A horned toad with goosebumps is one sorry sight!
But—no workin' with Billie, no sharin' the chili!"
Taffy shivered and skated away.

Finally, the chili was done. It smelled dee-licious!

Miss Billie took a taste. Her ears drooped. Her armadilly chili just wasn't right. It tasted flat as a Texas prairie.

She checked her recipe. She hadn't forgotten anything. What was wrong?

She looked around. Her kitchen was warm and bright and cozy. Outside the wind howled and whistled. Miss Billie peered out the window into the darkness. "I know what I forgot," she said.

Ding, dong! The doorbell rang again. Miss Billie opened the door.
Mackie, Tex, and Taffy stood in front of her.

She gasped. "Land sakes! Your noses are as blue as I feel!
What are you carrying there?"

"Sacks full of apologies," Tex said.

"Well, come on in," said Miss Billie.

"I brought a thermos of hot apple cider, for sipping with friends!" Mackie said.
"I brought hot jalapeño biscuits, for sopping with friends," Tex said.
"And I brought homemade chocolate fudge to sweeten us up," Taffy added.
Miss Billie hugged them all. "Friends—that's what my armadilly chili was missing!"

The four friends set the table together, then talked and laughed long into the cold, blustery night.

And the armadilly chili was perfect.

W24
A 10/10/05

10-05

E        Ketteman, Helen
         Armadilly chili.